Flamingo Court

LIFE IN THREE CONDOS

by Luigi Creatore

A SAMUEL FRENCH ACTING EDITION

SAMUEL FRENCH

FOUNDED 1830

NEW YORK HOLLYWOOD LONDON TORONTO

SAMUELFRENCH.COM

ISBN 978-0-573-69611-4   Printed in U.S.A.   #8711

IMPORTANT BILLING AND CREDIT
REQUIREMENTS

All producers of *FLAMINGO COURT* *must* give credit to the Author of the Play in all programs distributed in connection with performances of the Play, and in all instances in which the title of the Play appears for the purposes of advertising, publicizing or otherwise exploiting the Play and/or a production. The name of the Author *must* appear on a separate line on which no other name appears, immediately following the title and *must* appear in size of type not less than fifty percent of the size of the title type.

NEW WORLD STAGES

340 West 50th Street

Theatre 21
Carolyn Rossi Copeland
present

Jamie Farr   Anita Gillette

**Life in
Three Condos**

By
Luigi Creatore

with

Lucy Martin   Herbert Rubens   Joe Vincent

Set Design	Lighting Design	Costume Design	Sound Design
James Youmans	**Herrick Goldman**	**Carol Sherry**	**David A. Arnold**

Press	Casting	Production Manager
Keith Sherman & Associates	**Mark Simon**	**Aduro Productions**

Advertising	Production Stage Manager	General Management
Eliran Murphy Group	**Eileen F. Haggerty**	**CRC Productions/ Robert E. Schneider**

Directed by
Steven Yuhasz

The producers wish to express their appreciation to Theatre Development Fund for its support of this production.

CHARACTERS

ACT I

"ANGELINA"

Apartment 104

ANGELINA. Italian, caring, moved a year ago from Brooklyn.

MARIE. A matchmaker, nosey, abrupt, a trouble maker, says what she thinks. Angelina's neighbor and best friend.

DOMINIC. Italian. Sensitive, gullible. A man of honor. Romantic.

INTERMISSION

ACT II

"CLARA"

Apartment 204

CLARA. Gentle, firm, opinionated. She has early stage dementia.

ARTHUR. Her husband. To the point, strong direction, knows what he wants.

ACT III

"HARRY"

Apartment 304

HARRY ROSSOFF. Celebrating his eighty-ninth birthday. Determined, feisty, crusty character.

MARK SEAGAL. A hearing-aid salesman. Polite, honest, intelligent.

CHARITY PIPICK. Harry's daughter. Pushy, overbearing, controlling.

WALTER PIPICK. Charity's husband. A lawyer. Spineless, completely dominated by his wife.

CHI CHI. A hooker.

NOTE ON CASTING: Characters ages range from 60s to 89. 5 to 10 Actors may be used (depends on whether you want to double or triple roles or not)

SETTING

The time is the present; all of the action of the plays takes place in a three-story apartment complex in South Florida. Not a retirement village, but many retirees live there.

PRODUCTION NOTES

Flamingo Court was the name given to these three one act plays as a way to tie them together and clarify that all of these characters were residence of the same senior condo complex. We felt that by doing this the audience would be able to connect each of the stories of the plays, yet the plays would stand on their own. This "Life In Three Condos" is mostly the funny side of their lives, but also a moment to reflect as life changes. Each of these plays are to be approached in their style: "Angelina" is a sitcom, "Clara" is a realistic vignette and "Harry" is sketch comedy. Keep the moments and acting in each of these real, honest; the comedy will come from that.

The technical requirements can be as simple or sophisticated as your budget allows. The set was designed as the script requires; each play take place in a separate apartment. This allowed us to keep the same overall design and change the furniture and set dressing in between each of the acts to give a different feel. It also allowed for relatively fast changes between to the plays that were placed back to back.

Approaching the lighting differently in each of the acts helped in achieving a feeling of the varied environments of the occupants. Angelina's furniture was new, the room was bright with all of the action taking place during the day. For Clara and Arthur most everything in the condo was removed and it was very sparse, the action took place late in the afternoon during a thunder storm adding to the dim lighting and pulling the lighting to the center of the stage to focus on them. Arthur's apartment was a bachelor pad...he was 89; he had lived alone for many years. Piles of magazines, newspapers, sink full of dishes, golf clubs, fishing gear and trophies were dressed around the set.

Casting will also impact your set and costume designs, which depend on the number of actors that you cast in the show. There are ten different characters in the three plays, but the show can be done, as was done Off Broadway, with five actors. You can use between five and ten actors. With five actors we had the challenge of quick set and costume changes; this will affect your running crew size. In casting if you use five actors, two of those actors have to change from Clara and Arthur to whatever character you assign them in "Harry." Also, to note there are no specific actor tracks, so depending on your casting choices, role assignments are based on your talent.

From the moment I approached "Clara" conceptually I wanted to create a family photo album, a side show, projections of the memories of the lives of these two people. By doing this before the lights came up on them dancing for the last time, before the dialogue started, the audience had a sense or a connection with these two people as someone they could relate to or knew.

For the set change from "Clara" to "Harry" we needed time to cover for the set change. We had created for the original production "The Flamingo Court Flapper" which was a series of bulletin board announcements. The "Flapper was also projected with instrumental music underscoring, and moved it at the top of the set change. The one last thing we did was to use the song "Old Is In," written by our playwright, Luigi Creatore, as the Flamingo Court theme song; you will find this at the end of the script. This was recorded with all the cast members and used as a prerecorded voice over. This plays following the "Flapper" and was done as an audience sing along with them following the bouncing flamingo as the words flashed on the screen. In addition, since we had a screen that we flew in and out, we used it as a show emblem at the top of the show and intermission with "Flamingo Court" on it, then at the top of each of the sections we projected "Angelina," "Clara' and the "Harry" to further clarify to the audience that these were separate plays and not just a new scene. This all worked very effectively.

In addition, music played for transitions was a big part in the overall tone of the show; we selected classic vocalist recordings of the era of the lives of these people, from the 40's to the present. The music was all very upbeat and had lush orchestrations which provided a nostalgic familiarity for the audience, but also songs where picked for their lyric content and themes that introduced or tied up scenes or the acts and characters.

Have fun...laugh. It's good for you!

Steven Yuhasz
Off Broadway Director

ACT I
"Angelina"

Scene One

(Apartment 104. Angelina's one-bedroom apartment. The front door is stage right. Downstage right, there is a dining table and chairs and behind that a counter which separates the open kitchen from the dining area. Upstage center, there is a sofa facing upstage and two small chairs facing the sofa to create a seating area. Stage Left, the living room area is furnished with two comfortable chairs facing down stage. Two other doors are on the Stage Left wall. The Upstage door leads to the bedroom. The Downstage door leads to a closet. As the lights come up, ANGELINA is in the kitchen watching a counter top TV while stirring a pot of soup on the stove. The "Soap" dialogue in a VOICE OVER is heard by the audience and is as follows:)

PHILLIP. Don't stop me now, Marian. I've tried to tell you before…and now I've found the courage… you must let me go.

MARIAN. No, no, Phillip. It mustn't end like this.

PHILLIP. Listen to me, Marian…We both knew it had to end.

ANGELINA. *(not buying it)* Sure, *now* you say that…after you got what you wanted.

    MARIAN. If Edna won't give you the divorce, then we'll find another way…

PHILLIP. That doesn't sound like you.

ANGELINA. *(to TV)* You stink!

    MARIAN. I don't care. I don't care anymore.

ANGELINA. See what you are doing to her?

PHILLIP. I'm sorry, Marian, I'm sorry.

MARIAN. No, no!

PHILLIP. I must leave you.

(MUSIC comes up.)

ANGELINA. Don't you worry, sweetheart. He's not leaving.

*(As the episode ends, **ANGELINA** turns off the TV and crosses to the table with placemats. **MARIE** enters without knocking and crosses to the counter.)*

MARIE. Do you think Phillip is going to leave Marian?

ANGELINA. No.

MARIE. But he just said so. Weren't you watching?

ANGELINA. Of course I was watching. Would you put the dishes on the table, please?

*(**MARIE** takes dishes and silver from the counter and sets the table with three places.)*

ANGELINA. Phillip has said this before. It has been my experience that if a person keeps saying the same thing, they never do it. *(handing **MARIE** a platter)* Here's the bread. It's already sliced.

*(**DOMINIC** enters without knocking.)*

DOMINIC. Do you think Phillip is going to leave Marian?

ANGELINA. No.

MARIE. Tell him why.

ANGELINA. Well, my experience has been that if a person keeps saying he's going to do something, he never does it.

DOMINIC. Ah, you are so right, Angelina. I can see it now. He is absolutely not going to leave because he says he is. That is clear. *(beat)* On the other hand, if he keeps saying it, one day we may find out he really means it. I brought plum jam for the bread.

ANGELINA. That's very nice of you Dominic. It's my favorite. But you really shouldn't. You do too much. Yesterday it was chocolates, the day before it was bonbons.

*(***DOMINIC*** *takes a seat at the table.)*

MARIE. I didn't get any bonbons.

ANGELINA. We don't need all that, do we Marie?

*(***ANGELINA*** *sets a bowl of soup on a tray and carries it to the table.)*

MARIE. Why ask me? He brings all that stuff for you.

ANGELINA. Don't be silly, it's for all of us.

*(***ANGELINA*** *crosses to the counter and picks up an ornate peppermill.)*

DOMINIC. *(tastes the soup)* Needs salt. *(adds a bit of salt)*

MARIE. Maybe he can't have salt. Angie, can Frank have salt?

*(***ANGELINA*** *crosses to table and grinds a bit of pepper into the soup.)*

ANGELINA. I don't think it would hurt him. I do know he likes a bit of pepper.

DOMINIC. How is poor Frank today?

MARIE. Yes, how is your *husband* today?

ANGELINA. Well, he had a quiet night. That's about as much as I can say. *(She picks up tray with soup and crosses to bedroom door.)* I'd better bring him his soup before he gets restless. Later I'll make him a little pastina. Something he can digest easily.

(She exits into the bedroom with the soup.)

DOMINIC. Isn't she wonderful? So caring....you might say noble.

MARIE. And beautiful.

DOMINIC. Ahhh, beautiful! Yes, beautiful, beautiful!

MARIE. I don't think she's that beautiful.

DOMINIC. That's because you don't see her as a man does. When she walks across the room, standing proud and lovely, swaying just a bit...did I say swaying?...undulating! I tell you she can set a man on fire.

MARIE. You ought to be ashamed of yourself. I see you making goo-goo eyes at her, and bringing little presents, and running errands for her. The whole building's been talking about it.

DOMINIC. They're just gossips.

MARIE. Sure, and with you running after a woman whose husband has been sick in bed since the day she moved in, you've handed them a real spicy meatball to chew on.

DOMINIC. I can't help it, Marie. I've tried to suppress my feelings for this...for this angel, but I can't. After my wife died I thought I'd never feel this way about another woman. I don't know what to do.

MARIE. *(pouring coffee for both)* Have some coffee.

DOMINIC. Advise me, Marie.

MARIE. Have some bread and forget about it. That's my advice.

*(**DOMINIC** picks up a slice of bread and smells it.)*

DOMINIC. Ah, it's wonderful. And light. And beautiful, just the way she is. You know Angelina makes the bread with her own hands?

MARIE. Because she wants her husband, Frank, to have fresh bread.

DOMINIC. Don't torture me like this.

MARIE. Oh my, you are in bad shape.

DOMINIC. You don't know the half of it. The other night I dreamt I killed him.

MARIE. Killed who?

DOMINIC. *(pointing to bedroom)* Him. Him, in there. Frank. I dreamt I killed him. I woke up in a sweat...my whole body trembling. I didn't know this head could have such thoughts.

MARIE. Be careful, those are the kind of thoughts God punishes.

DOMINIC. I know...and I want to fall on my knees and beg God forgiveness for these terrible ideas that come into my mind. On the other hand…God gave me my mind, it is He who makes it function. So He must bear some of the responsibility for my thoughts.

MARIE. I've never heard such a crock.

DOMINIC. A crock? Then you're saying that you don't believe me? I'm a liar? You're calling me, Dominic Sevanti, a liar?

(ANGELINA enters with the tray and soup bowl, now empty, and places it on the kitchen counter.)

DOMINIC. I would like to announce here and now, that I am not a liar, I don't respect liars, I don't and would not associate with anyone who is a liar and that's for now and always!

ANGELINA. You mustn't get so excited, Dominic. It's bad for your health. Now…I want you to calm down, take a deep breath,…and think pleasant thoughts.

(DOMINIC takes a deep breath and exhales, making a lover's sigh)

DOMINIC. Ahhhhh, Angelina, you know exactly how to calm me down.

MARIE. That's not the way I heard it.

ANGELINA. *(to DOMINIC)* May I pour you some more coffee?

DOMINIC. No thank you. But allow me to pour for you. *(He does so.)*

MARIE. *(looking around)* Did you get the paper today, Angie?

DOMINIC. Please don't call her Angie. Her name is Angelina. It means little angel. Angie sounds like a heart condition.

MARIE. Did you get the paper?

ANGELINA. No. And today's the second day they didn't deliver. I don't know what's the matter with them. I'm lost without my paper.

DOMINIC. Why didn't you say something? *(rising)* I'll go out immediately and get you your newspaper.

ANGELINA. You don't have to bother. Besides, the nearest place is all the way to Military.

DOMINIC. It's not that far. I'll walk. It does me good to walk. Keeps the old body trim.

ANGELINA. Well, thank you Dominic. You're very kind.

DOMINIC. Ta, ta.

ANGELINA. Ta, ta.

    (**DOMINIC** *exits.*)

MARIE. *(after* **DOMINIC** *is gone)* Ta, ta. Ta, ta. What kind of way is that for grown people to talk? What's going on here?

ANGELINA. There's nothing "going on."

MARIE. *(mocking again)* Ta ta, ta ta?

ANGELINA. Well…there may be an attraction…of sorts. But, under the circumstances….

MARIE. Reminds me of a rooster pecking around a nice juicy hen.

ANGELINA. What do you know about roosters and hens?

MARIE. I spent one summer on a farm when I was little. I remember watching this rooster circling and pecking around this hen. Now the hen makes out like she doesn't know he's there. Only…once in a while she gives him a look…And all of a sudden this big rooster pounces, and bang! – they're making eggs.

ANGELINA. Marie, I have to talk to you…

MARIE. Uh huh.

ANGELINA. There's something I have to tell you…

MARIE. Uh huh.

ANGELINA. But first I have to swear you to secrecy.

MARIE. I swear.

ANGELINA. Too easy. I want you to mean it.

MARIE. I mean it.

ANGELINA. Raise your right hand.

    (**MARIE** *raises hand.*)

    I swear I will never reveal –

MARIE. I swear I will never reveal –

ANGELINA....what my dear friend, Angelina, is about to tell me.

MARIE....what my dear friend Angie – Angelina is about to tell me.

ANGELINA. Let me see your left hand.

(MARIE brings it up to eye level.)

Your fingers are crossed.

MARIE. That's just in case of an emergency. I swear to you I won't tell. *(holding up both hands)* Look, both hands.

ANGELINA. All right, I'm going to trust you. But...this is very difficult for me –

MARIE. *(guesses)* You did it! You did it already! And, behind my back!

ANGELINA. What are you talking about? Did what?

MARIE. *(tapping the first finger of each hand together)* You and the rooster...you know.

ANGELINA. No, I *don't* know. You're talking nonsense.

MARIE. Oh, am I? You said yourself you were attracted to him.

ANGELINA. Well, I am. But that's not what I want to talk to you about. I want to talk to you about...about Frank.

MARIE. Your husband?

ANGELINA. My husband, Frank. Yes. Marie, I don't know any other way to say this but to...to just say it...

MARIE. Well, go ahead already, I can't stand it.

ANGELINA. Frank is dead.

MARIE. Frank is dead. Frank is dead. When did this happen?

ANGELINA. Two years ago.

MARIE. Two years. You mean before you moved here?

ANGELINA. Oh yes. Well before I moved here.

MARIE. Well, who's in the bedroom?

ANGELINA. There's nobody in the bedroom.

MARIE. Nobody?

ANGELINA. Nobody.

(**MARIE** *exits into bedroom and re-appears almost immediately.*)

MARIE. There's nobody in the bedroom! Would you tell me – what the hell's going on here?

ANGELINA. That's what I'm trying to do. Sit down, Marie.

(**MARIE** *sits as* **ANGELINA** *paces and tells the story.*)

ANGELINA. Frank died two years ago in Brooklyn. I went through a funeral you wouldn't believe. Relatives came from all over. Friends stayed with me, held my hand, fed me…they couldn't do enough for me. The minute the funeral was over so was all the attention and the promises.

MARIE. I know. I've been through it.

ANGELINA. And there I was all alone in this big house – we never had children, you know. I was getting to know the meaning of lonely. That's when I sold the house and moved down here.

MARIE. To get a new start.

ANGELINA. Yes. To make new friends and get a new start.

MARIE. *(indicating the bedroom)* So how did this happen?

ANGELINA. It was my first day in Florida. I hadn't even unpacked…and I went down to the pool for my first swim. Well, I met Mrs. Rittman – you know her –

MARIE. Yeah, big mouth Rittman.

ANGELINA. So she's sitting there *with* her husband – since Frank died it seems everyone has a husband but me – and she says, "Welcome to Paradise," and I say, "Thank you," and then she says, "Are you alone?" And, I don't know why, but I said, "No, I'm with my husband." And she says, "Oh, is he going to join us for a swim?" And I said, "No, he's sick. He's in bed." It was a stupid thing to say, but I said it. And before I knew it, Rittman was telling everyone about the "new couple" in 104.

MARIE. Some buildings have little newspapers they put out. We've got big mouth Rittman.

ANGELINA. Then the word got out that Frank was terminally ill and I was being brave.

MARIE. I remember that.

ANGELINA. Yes, that's when you came around – God bless you – and offered your help. I knew you'd be my friend.

MARIE. Some friend. I helped you baby-sit an empty room. *(suddenly remembering)* The soup!

ANGELINA. What about the soup?

MARIE. What do you do with it?

ANGELINA. Throw it in the toilet.

MARIE. And you put a pinch of pepper in it every day?

ANGELINA. Yes, I thought it was a nice touch.

MARIE. There's a lot I don't know about you.

ANGELINA. Then one day you brought Dominic to share our coffee.

MARIE. Oh my God, Dominic!

ANGELINA. What about Dominic?

MARIE. Wait till he finds out!

ANGELINA. Dominic is not going to find out, because I'm not going to tell him. And you are sworn to secrecy.

MARIE. Ayi, I knew I shouldn't have put up both hands.

ANGELINA. Besides, Dominic would not take this very well. He is a man of honor. He hates liars. Give me advice.

MARIE. All right. My advice is…let's tell him!

ANGELINA. I say no.

MARIE. I can't wait to see his face. I say tell him.

ANGELINA. I say no.

MARIE. I say yes.

ANGELINA. You swore – with both hands.

(**DOMINIC** *enters with newspaper*)

DOMINIC. There you are Angelina. Now you won't be lost. So…what are we talking about?

MARIE & ANGELINA. *(exchange a look)* Nothing.

(BLACKOUT)

Scene Two

(The next day. The television is on, volume is turned up.)

PHILLIP. I don't know how you can be so good to me. I must have done something wonderful in another life to deserve someone like you.

ANGELINA. Here we go again!

MARIAN. Phillip, when two people love each other the way we do, there is nothing…no force on earth that can keep us apart.

ANGELINA. But you can't trust him. I told you that.

PHILLIP. And to think I lied to you. The one thing I can't forgive myself is for having lied to you.

ANGELINA. Give me a break!

MARIAN. Well, if *you* can't forgive yourself, I can.

PHILLIP. You are wonderful, my darling, but, my children are the innocent victims of all this. It's the children I have to think about.

ANGELINA. Why didn't you think about that before you unzipped your pants, big shot!

*(Music up and out as **ANGELINA** turns the TV off. **MARIE** enters without knocking.)*

MARIE. That Marian is going to be the death of me. Why should she take Phillip back after the way he acted?

ANGELINA. I told you he wouldn't leave. And she's taking him back, the way I see it, because she's in an impossible situation. I knew this would happen.

MARIE. Speaking of people who paint themselves into corners – what's *your* next move.

ANGELINA. I don't know. I've been thinking – but I just don't know. I seem to have the answers to the Soap all right. But when it comes to my own life…

MARIE. Listen, Angie, why don't you tell Dominic the truth?

ANGELINA. I can't do that.

MARIE. Yes you can.

ANGELINA. No I can't. Did you tell him? Did you say something to him?

MARIE. Hey, I'm sworn! I can't do a thing. But I think you should tell him. And you know what? I'll bet he would understand.

ANGELINA. You think so?

MARIE. Sure I think so.

(**DOMINIC** *enters without knocking.*)

DOMINIC. Can you imagine Marian taking Phillip back like that?

MARIE. Angelina said she would.

DOMINIC. *(to ANGELINA)* How would you figure that? Phillip lied to her. How could she ever trust him again?

ANGELINA. He had to...to tell her a few falsehoods. But I don't think he lied that much...

DOMINIC. Ah, my dear Angelina, how could you know about such things? You are so pure and honest...not a deceitful thought would enter your mind. That's why I...I respect you so much. But that Phillip...I tell you he is a liar. And I...*hate*...liars.

ANGELINA. Yes. Well...thank goodness it's only a television story, eh? Now sit down and have some coffee.

(**DOMINIC** *and* **MARIE** *sit at the table as* **ANGELINA** *pours coffee.*)

DOMINIC. I didn't bring anything today. I'm sorry.

ANGELINA. Don't be silly. I told you, you do too much for me...us. I have some of the plum jam from yesterday, if you'd like.

MARIE. How about some of those chocolates Dom brought the day before.

ANGELINA. I don't think there are any more.

MARIE. But we must have left half the box.

ANGELINA. Frank ate them.

(**ANGELINA** *crosses to get the pepper mill and soup tray.* **DOMINIC** *puts dash of salt in the soup as she puts pepper in the soup.*)

MARIE. How did Frank like them?

ANGELINA. He liked them just fine. Let me just bring him his soup so he doesn't get nervous.

(She exits into the bedroom with the soup.)

DOMINIC. God bless that Frank. He's got a good appetite. You know, I love that man in there. I never met him, and yet I love him. You know why? Because she loves him. That's why I love him. On the other hand, I hate him! He stands between me and my Angelina. He causes me sleepless nights – and pain…oh the pain. And then, I want to kill him – actually kill him…put poison in his soup. Is that terrible of me, Marie?

*(Long pause as **MARIE** stares into space.)*

Marie?

MARIE. I'm thinking, I'm thinking.

DOMINIC. What is there to think about – I'm a terrible person.

MARIE. Don't be so hard on yourself – nobody's perfect.

DOMINIC. Perhaps you're right. We all have our flaws, our little peccadillos. That is, with the exception of Angelina.

MARIE. Not so fast, Dominic.

DOMINIC. What do you mean?

MARIE. I mean, nobody's perfect. And that includes your precious Angelina.

DOMINIC. You're just jealous of her. You can't point out one imperfection, one flaw in that good lady's character.

MARIE. Oh, no?

DOMINIC. No.

MARIE. Well, what if I were to tell you that Frank – that Frank didn't eat the chocolates. Angelina did.

DOMINIC. So what if she shared a few chocolates with Frank?

MARIE. And what about the cannoli? She knew they were my favorite. And she says Frank ate them.

DOMINIC. I don't understand.

MARIE. He didn't eat them. She ate them.

DOMINIC. What are you talking about?

MARIE. I'm not at liberty to say.

DOMINIC. This is nonsense.

MARIE. It's not nonsense.

DOMINIC. It's nonsense and it's ridiculous.

> (**ANGELINA** *enters and crosses to place tray with empty soup bowl on kitchen counter, then sits at table.*)

ANGELINA. What's ridiculous?

DOMINIC. We were talking about the Soap. You know it gets more ridiculous every day. I don't know why we watch it.

ANGELINA. I suppose it fills an hour of our lives – and gives us something to talk about.

DOMINIC. I can think of other things to talk about.

MARIE. Let's talk about Frank.

ANGELINA. I'd rather not.

MARIE. Why not?

ANGELINA. This is the only time I have to relax – when I sit down with my friends and have a cup of coffee and I really don't want to talk about – the sickness.

DOMINIC. *(to* **MARIE***)* She's right. Now, may we respect the lady's wishes?

MARIE. You respect her wishes, I have to go. *(She crosses to front door.)*

ANGELINA. Oh? Where are you going?

MARIE. I'm meeting the girls and we're going Mall hopping and shopping. Ta, ta!

> (**MARIE** *exits.*)

DOMINIC. She's some gem, that one.

ANGELINA. Oh, but she's a good soul.

DOMINIC. Sometimes she carries on like she's demented. She doesn't make any sense.

ANGELINA. But with it all, she's a good soul.

DOMINIC. You know what she told me? She told me you don't give Frank any chocolates or pastry. She says you eat them all yourself.

ANGELINA. She said that?

DOMINIC. And when I asked her why she would think such a thing, she says, "I'm not a liberty to say."

Oh, and I didn't tell you – the other day I passed her apartment and her door was open and she was sitting there actually talking to the television.

ANGELINA. No!

DOMINIC. Yes. Sometimes I think she's going crazy. And you sit – so generous, so kind – calling her a good soul.

ANGELINA. Well, maybe we're both right – she's a good soul who is going crazy. And under those circumstances, you can't believe anything she says.

DOMINIC. Exactly. And then, there's this obsession she's developing to continually talk about Frank. I know – everybody knows – how devoted you are to Frank. But even an angel of mercy has a right to relax.

(DOMINIC *rises and crosses behind* ANGELINA*'s chair placing his hands on her shoulders and massages her.*)

DOMINIC. How's that?

ANGELINA. Oh, that's nice. Very nice.

DOMINIC. First your body relaxes, then your mind relaxes. Someday, my dear Angelina, these troubles will be over, and I'm going to take you with me.

ANGELINA. Oh? And where are you going to take me?

DOMINIC. To Italy. To Roma. Did I tell you I was born in Rome? Of course, we came to America when I was only a child. Still, I feel I'm a Roman.

ANGELINA. I was born here. But my parents came from Naples.

DOMINIC. Ah, you can see it. The warmth…the heart…the devotion to family – that's Neapolitan. And I'm going to take you to Naples too. But first, we go to my Roma.

(DOMINIC extends his hand. ANGELINA takes it, and they walk downstage.)

DOMINIC. Come, come. Here we are strolling down the Via Veneto. There are people from all over the world strolling ahead of us – behind us. The sidewalk tables are full of couples…most of them people-watching. See, they are watching us just as we are watching them. It's a favorite Roman pastime. That couple over there – they have eyes only for each other.

ANGELINA. They're young and they're in love.

DOMINIC. Ah, you can see that. And look – over there – isn't that the Italian movie star…a…what's-his-name-?

ANGELINA. Mastroiani.

DOMINIC. That's him.

ANGELINA. I thought he died.

DOMINIC. In Italy, old actors never die – they just hang around the Via Veneto sipping coffee. *(waves)* Hey, Marcello!

ANGELINA. He's waving back at you.

DOMINIC. That's because he sees you. He still has an eye for a pretty lady.

ANGELINA. What an eye – he's looking at an old lady…

DOMINIC. No, no, no. He sees you as I do. You're a pretty lady. Here, you with the flowers – a rose for La Signora.

(DOMINIC mimes buying a flower from a vendor and presents it to ANGELINA.)

DOMINIC. For you – and the rose blushes with shame to be in your presence.

ANGELINA. Oh my, are you always so romantic?

DOMINIC. When I'm in Rome – well, I can't help myself. Ah, here we are at Doney's Café. To my mind, the best on the Veneto. Wait till you taste their coffee laced with Belgian chocolate. Waiter – a table for two please. No, not out here with the tourists….we'll have a settee in one of the private booths. Away from the noise, if you don't mind. Ah, this is perfect.

(DOMINIC leads ANGELINA to the couch.)

DOMINIC. This is what I want for you. I want – someday – to take you away from all your cares. Tell me there is hope – tell me.

ANGELINA. Hush. We can't talk like this. What would you think of me if I did answer you?

DOMINIC. What do you mean, my sweet?

ANGELINA. I mean you wouldn't think very much of me if I engaged in this conversation with you with Frank in the next –

DOMINIC. No, no, no. We are in Rome. There is no Frank.

ANGELINA. But we are not in Rome.

DOMINIC. Angelina, please hold still one little minute.

(He puts his hands on her cheek, draws closer to her.)

With your permission. *(He kisses her.)*

ANGELINA. That was not with my permission. I want you to understand that.

DOMINIC. Yes, I understand. No permission. *(He kisses her again.)*

ANGELINA. That's enough now. I said enough! Stop with the hands.

DOMINIC. No…no. Nothing is enough! It's impossible to get enough of you.

(He presses towards her.)

ANGELINA. You ought to be ashamed of yourself. With my husband lying in the next room.

DOMINIC. I know, I know.

ANGELINA. Maybe on his death bed.

DOMINIC. You're right. I am ashamed. So ashamed…On the other hand, I can't help myself.

(DOMINIC and ANGELINA sink down on the couch.)

I tell you Angelina, I haven't felt this way in years…and years…and years…

(MARIE enters hurriedly from the front door, getting a full view of the couple on the couch.)

MARIE. Oh I forgot that –

DOMINIC. *(overlapping)* Oh Angelina!

ANGELINA. Oh Dominic!

MARIE. Oh my God – they're making eggs!

(MARIE exits, slamming door. ANGELINA and DOMINIC re-appear by sitting up on sofa, then cross downstage.)

ANGELINA. Marie! What do we do now?

DOMINIC. Angelina.

ANGELINA. She saw us!

DOMINIC. We have to talk.

ANGELINA. I can't talk now. I know what I have to do. *(crosses toward kitchen)* I have to put the bread in the oven.

DOMINIC. *(following her)* Let me help you.

ANGELINA. I don't need your help. You'll only get in my way. I still have to take care of this house. I still have to take care of my husband.

DOMINIC. And I want to take care of you. Listen to me, Angelina. I love you.

(They stop and stare at each other for a beat.)

Yes I do. And I can change your life and mine –

ANGELINA. But how? What –

DOMINIC. Shh…I *will* change your life and mine, if you say the word. You must tell me if there is hope – hope, you understand – that you may love me too.

ANGELINA. There is…more than hope.

DOMINIC. Oh, you make me happy. Happy, happy, happy.

ANGELINA. *(picking up pan with dough)* Let's not talk about it anymore. I need time to think. Right now I have to put the bread in to bake.

DOMINIC. *(taking the pan)* Here, I said I'd help.

ANGELINA. All right, but don't burn yourself. I'll hold the oven door open and you put the pan on the middle shelf. Do it right away, I don't want to lose the heat.

(ANGELINA bends over and opens the oven door as the front door opens and MARIE enters. MARIE cannot see ANGELINA and DOMINIC.)

MARIE. Is it safe to come in?

ANGELINA. Hurry up, Dominic. Stick it in.

> (**MARIE** *exits, slamming door, as* **ANGELINA** *and* **DOMINIC** *reappear, looking toward door.*)
>
> (*BLACKOUT*)

Scene 3

(It is the next afternoon. ANGELINA is at kitchen counter. There is a knock on the door.)

ANGELINA. Come in.

(MARIE enters, looking around.)

ANGELINA. Since when do you knock?

MARIE. Since yesterday at three thirty-six P.M.

ANGELINA. You noticed the exact time?

MARIE. I didn't have anything else to do.

ANGELINA. How was the Mall hopping and shopping?

MARIE. I didn't go. There was a hellava lot more action right here. Is there anything you want to tell me?

ANGELINA. There is nothing to tell. I really don't want to talk about this.

MARIE. Alright, we won't talk about this. Let's talk about the soap. Do you think Marian's pregnant?

ANGELINA. I don't know –

(DOMINIC enters. DOMINIC and ANGELINA have eye contact for a beat, then break.)

ANGELINA. ...ask Dominic what he thinks...I have to go give Frank his pill.

(She exits into the bedroom.)

DOMINIC. Ask Dominic what?

MARIE. About the Soap.

DOMINIC. I didn't watch today. I didn't sleep a moment last night. And then this morning I was busy making certain purchases. This isn't easy, but it must be done. I don't care what price I may have to pay – *(looking up)* later.

MARIE. What are you talking about?

DOMINIC. Better you don't know. I can only say this – There is a tide in the affairs of men which, when taken at the flood, leads on to fortune.

MARIE. What the hell is that?

(**ANGELINA** *enters, crosses to kitchen, brings tray with soup to table and crosses to get pepper mill.*)

ANGELINA. That's Shakespeare. I didn't know you were a student of Shakespeare, Dominic.

DOMINIC. One of my many hidden qualities.

DOMINIC. *(to **MARIE**)* Would you get the bread please?

(*As **MARIE** crosses to counter, **DOMINIC** takes a small bottle out of his pocket and pours a dark liquid into the soup. **ANGELINA** does not see this. **MARIE** turns in time to see the action. Reacts by looking towards the bedroom turning to say something to **ANGELINA** but stopping herself - finally sitting at table.*)

ANGELINA. *(putting pepper into soup)* One, two, three. Mustn't put too much in.

MARIE. We wouldn't want to upset Frank's stomach, would we?

ANGELINA. No we wouldn't.

(**ANGELINA** *picks up tray and exits into bedroom.*)

MARIE. *(pouring coffee)* So what did you put in Frank's soup today – Soy Sauce?

DOMINIC. *(very nervous)* I don't know what you are talking about.

MARIE. I saw you.

DOMINIC. Ah, the Soy Sauce. Yes, I thought a dash of Soy Sauce…instead of salt you know. Too much salt is bad for the liver.

MARIE. I know what you did.

DOMINIC. You do?

MARIE. You put poison in the soup.

DOMINIC. Don't say that.

MARIE. What did you use?

DOMINIC. Rat and weed killer. Are you going to turn me in?

MARIE. No. Strange as it may seem, Dominic – I'm on your side.

DOMINIC. You are? Then help me get through this. I think I'm going to explode right here.

MARIE. Drink some coffee.

DOMINIC. You're such a friend, Marie. Such a friend. I'll never say another word against you as long as I live. How long do you think it'll take Frank to finish his soup?

*(**DOMINIC** picks up his cup, rattling it, then sipping.)*

MARIE. About as long as it takes you to finish your coffee.

DOMINIC. *(noisily putting the cup down)* I don't think I can stay.

MARIE. You'll stay. I'm not going to go through this alone.

DOMINIC. But *you* didn't do anything.

MARIE. Are you kidding? I'm the accomplice.

DOMINIC. Ah yes, and a wonderful accomplice. I'm surrounded by wonderful people…you, Angelina –

MARIE. Frank.

DOMINIC. Yes, Frank. He is wonderful. I've said that myself. What was I thinking of? We can't do this, Marie.

MARIE. We already did it, Dominic.

DOMINIC. *(rising and crossing toward bedroom door)* Maybe it's not too late. I've got to stop it.

MARIE. I wouldn't do that if I were you.

DOMINIC. I've got to try.

*(**ANGELINA** enters from bedroom carrying tray with empty bowl, collides with **DOMINIC** and drops tray.)*

DOMINIC. Oh, I'm sorry, I'm sorry. Let me –

ANGELINA. *(picking up bowl and tray)* That's alright. I've got it.

DOMINIC. Did I get any on you?

ANGELINA. No, the bowl is empty. See?

DOMINIC. Then he finished it all?

ANGELINA. Yes, of course.

MARIE. How did he like it?

ANGELINA. He liked it fine. What's all this interest in
Frank's soup?

MARIE. Dominic added a dash of Soy Sauce to it – instead
of salt he says.

ANGELINA. Well, thank you Dominic. That's very sweet
of you. Yes, Frank seemed to like it particularly well
today.

DOMINIC. I have to go. *(to* **MARIE***)* Is it alright if I go now?

ANGELINA. What are you asking her for?

DOMINIC. I don't know.

ANGELINA. But we haven't had our visit yet. Have you had
your coffee?

DOMINIC. Have to go. Sick. That's it, I'm sick.

*(***DOMINIC** *exits quickly.)*

ANGELINA. What's the matter with him?

MARIE. I didn't notice anything.

ANGELINA. Do you suppose he's nervous about – about
yesterday?

MARIE. I think he's nervous about today.

ANGELINA. Marie, you're my best friend. You know everything about me. You're the only one I can turn to. I
don't know what to do. I don't know what's going to
happen next.

MARIE. I'll tell you what's going to happen next. Tonight,
Frank is going to die.

(BLACKOUT)

Scene 4

(It is the next morning. ANGELINA *is seated at the table having a cup of coffee. She is dressed in black.* MARIE *bursts in.)*

MARIE. I told him.

ANGELINA. You told him. What did he say?

MARIE. Nothing. He just sort of turned purple and white, and then he started throwing up. Hey, the dress is perfect. Where'd you get it?

ANGELINA. I had it left over from two years ago.

MARIE. From the last time Frank died.

(She takes medicine bottles from a small bag and spreads them on the table.)

I bought some over-the-counter sedatives for you.

ANGELINA. I don't need any sedatives.

MARIE. I know, but it's a good touch. Like grinding pepper into the soup.

(There is a knock on the door.)

ANGELINA. Oh my God. He's here already. Answer the door. No. Take this cup. I shouldn't have anything. I'm so nervous. I hope I say the right thing.

MARIE. Don't worry. If you don't know what to say – cry.

*(*MARIE *answers the door,* DOMINIC *enters.)*

DOMINIC. Marie just told me what happened. I'm so sorry.

*(*ANGELINA *cries loudly, then stops herself with her handkerchief)*

ANGELINA. He loved you. Did you know that? Frank loved you.

DOMINIC. And we all loved him. I was just saying that to Marie yesterday. Right Marie?

MARIE. Yep. It was just after you put the Soy Sauce in his soup.

DOMINIC. But when did this happen? Why didn't you call me?

ANGELINA. It was the middle of the night.

DOMINIC. I would have come.

ANGELINA. No, no. It was something I had to do alone. I called the undertaker – and within an hour or so it was all over. Frank was gone.

DOMINIC. *(to* **MARIE***)* An angel. An angel to the end. *(to* **ANGELINA***)* Where did they take him?

ANGELINA. What?

DOMINIC. Where did they take him?

(**ANGELINA** *starts crying loudly. Looks to* **MARIE** *–* **MARIE** *shrugs.)*

ANGELINA. Heaven! They…they took him to heaven.

DOMINIC. Before that. What's the name of the funeral parlor? I have to take you there. The neighbors will want to send flowers.

ANGELINA. No! No flowers. Frank didn't want flowers. He's allergic to flowers. See, he arranged everything himself. He didn't want me to worry.

DOMINIC. And where did they take him?

ANGELINA. Right now he's in a plane heading for Brooklyn. He'll be buried in the family plot.

DOMINIC. Are you telling me you're not going to the funeral?

(**ANGELINA** *starts crying and looks to* **MARIE** *for help.)*

MARIE. Are you telling us that Frank didn't want you to go to the funeral?

ANGELINA. That's the way Frank wanted it. He said, "When I die, I don't want flowers and I don't want you to come to my funeral. Everything has been arranged. They will take me to Brooklyn and bury me in the family plot. I'll wait for you there." And then he said, "Don't hurry."

DOMINIC. What a wonderful man.

MARIE. Did he say he wanted you to remarry and have a good life because you were so much younger than he was?

ANGELINA. Yes, he did.

DOMINIC. Marie, may I ask you to leave us for a little while? I think I can bring some consolation to our dear friend.

MARIE. I don't mind at all. I have shopping to do. *(exiting)* When I come back, I'll knock.

DOMINIC. Angelina, I know you've been under a strain for a long time. And last night must have been awful for you. And I know this is not the proper time to speak of such things – on the other hand, it may bring you some comfort to know that I am waiting, whenever you think the time has arrived, to ask for your hand in marriage.

ANGELINA. Yes.

DOMINIC. Yes?

ANGELINA. Yes.

DOMINIC. This is fantastic. Fantastic. I'm going to start planning our honeymoon. Oh, I know we'll have to wait for a decent period of mourning. But then, we're really going to Rome. And Naples – I promised you Naples. Now, there's another thing. There's a corner apartment coming up for sale. You could decorate it, and it would be a fresh start for both of us. Angelina? Are you listening? What's the matter?

ANGELINA. It's no good. I can't do it.

DOMINIC. Can't do what.

ANGELINA. I can't marry you. Not now, not ever.

DOMINIC. This is nonsense. This is just some reaction you're having.

ANGELINA. Listen to me, Dominic. When people our age marry, it should be for the rest of their lives.

DOMINIC. Of course. We're going to spend the rest of our lives together.

ANGELINA. And that kind of a beautiful relationship can't be built on deceit and lies.

DOMINIC. Deceit and lies? What did Marie tell you? I didn't do it.

ANGELINA. Marie didn't tell me anything. I'm talking about something I did.

DOMINIC. That you did?

ANGELINA. I've done a terrible thing –

DOMINIC. *(speaking to a child)* You know, you're right. Lies and deception – that's no way to start a marriage. Why don't you tell me this terrible thing that you've done and let me be the judge?

ANGELINA. Very well. But don't interrupt me, because I have to say it quickly. And after you hear this, I don't know that you can ever forgive me. Frank died two years ago in Brooklyn.

DOMINIC. What?

ANGELINA. I lied, I lied, I lied! Oh, how I lied! You see, when I came down here, I fell into a trap. I told some people my husband was with me, but sick in bed. They spread the word, and pretty soon the trap was closed tight. I had no way to get out.

DOMINIC. You mean there was no Frank? There was nobody in there?

ANGELINA. That's right.

DOMINIC. That's the damnedest thing I ever heard! On the other hand – it's also the greatest thing I ever heard. *(He starts laughing.)*

ANGELINA. What's so funny?

DOMINIC. I killed him. I killed Frank.

ANGELINA. How could you do that?

DOMINIC. I put poison in his soup. Oh my God, what did you do with the soup?

ANGELINA. I flushed it down the toilet.

DOMINIC. Perfect. And all our troubles went down with it. Now, we don't have to wait to get married. There *is* no Frank who died in the middle of the night, nothing to stop us. And you ask if I can ever forgive you. I forgive you with all my heart.

*(**DOMINIC** moves towards **ANGELINA** to embrace her.)*

ANGELINA. Get away from me.

DOMINIC. What's the matter?

ANGELINA. Do you think I could marry you now? You're a murderer.

DOMINIC. What are you saying?

ANGELINA. Murderer! Assassino!

DOMINIC. Angelina...

ANGELINA. Don't you touch me.

DOMINIC. Angelina, I can't believe what you're doing.

ANGELINA. I can't believe what you did to me. First you treat me like a plaything – while my husband is lying on his death bed. Then – then, in cold blood, you murder him.

DOMINIC. But there was nobody there. Nobody in the other room. Nobody on his death bed.

ANGELINA. Ah, but you didn't know that.

DOMINIC. And why didn't I know that? Because you lied to me, that's why. You made up a man who lived in the other room, and you drove me crazy with him. If you hadn't lied to me, I wouldn't have killed him.

ANGELINA. Oh, so now it's my fault.

DOMINIC. It certainly is.

ANGELINA. *(with deceptive calm)* What kind of poison did you use?

DOMINIC. Rat and weed killer.

ANGELINA. And you put it in the soup?

DOMINIC. Yes.

ANGELINA. ASS-ASS-INO! Get out! I don't want to marry you – I don't want to talk to you – I don't ever want to see you again. I'm only happy that I found out about you in time.

DOMINIC. That goes two ways. I tell you, Angelina, you're not only a liar, you're a cheat, and a strumpet and a loudmouth and a bitch. And *that's* Neapolitan. I wouldn't marry you –

(**MARIE** *bursts in.*)

MARIE. Hold it! I hope you kids aren't saying something you'll be sorry for later.

ANGELINA. What are you doing here?

MARIE. I got tired standing on the other side of the door listening. *(mocking)* Murderer – assassino – strumpet – bitch. These are not kind words. What's the matter with you dummies? So you both did things that were not quite on the up and up. But now you've got a chance to forget all that and maybe make both your lives a little better. What am I saying? – a lot better. And you're gonna blow it because of those Italian tempers?

DOMINIC. Marie, it's really none –

MARIE. Don't talk –

DOMINIC. Okay.

MARIE. *(overlapping)* – or I'll blow my stack and then you'll really see an Italian Fourth of July. Now, I'm going outside, and I want to hear all nice things come floating through that door. And remember, not many people get the chance you've got right now. Look around you.

(MARIE exits)

DOMINIC. *(to closed door)* Busybody.

ANGELINA. *(to same)* Know-it-all.

DOMINIC. Meddler.

ANGELINA. Matchmaker.

DOMINIC. *(to ANGELINA)* Matchmaker?

ANGELINA. Yes. She's right, you know. About us.

DOMINIC. In my heart, I know she is.

ANGELINA. You know, we don't have that many more years left that we can afford to waste them.

DOMINIC. I know. Come with me.

(DOMINIC takes ANGELINA's hand and leads her to chair, where they sit.)

ANGELINA. Are we in Rome?

DOMINIC. No, just home. Where we belong. And I want to ask you again – if it's just a few years we have left – will you spend them with me?

ANGELINA. Yes, my love.

(They kiss.)

DOMINIC. On the other hand, who's to say? It could be years...and years...

ANGELINA. And years and years.

(as the lights fade)

ANGELINA. Stop with the hands.

DOMINIC. Oh Angelina!

(BLACKOUT)

Intermission

ACT II
"Clara"

*(Apartment 204. Change of furniture. As the LIGHTS come up, MUSIC plays as we see **CLARA & ARTHUR BART-LEY** dancing very close as they have done for many years together. She is dressed simply, but in expectation of going someplace with a hat on. As the music stops, **ARTHUR** helps **CLARA** to sit on the Living room sofa. **ARTHUR** crosses to a side table, stares into the drawer. then closes it. He crosses to the window and looks out. **CLARA** calls.)*

CLARA. Arthur…Arthur…

ARTHUR. Yes, yes. What is it?

*(**ARTHUR** crosses to the sofa, sits.)*

CLARA. I just didn't know where you'd gone to.

ARTHUR. I'm here. I'm right here.

CLARA. *(Her hand discovers the hat she is wearing.)* Why am I wearing a hat?

ARTHUR. I told you, you're going to…Today's the day you're going…

CLARA. Why am I wearing a hat, Arthur? Can't you just answer a simple question?

ARTHUR. They're coming to take you to the Home. That's what we're waiting for.

CLARA. I'm not going to a Home. No siree, and no way Jose. And another thing…if you had any such thoughts – any such thoughts, Arthur, you certainly should have discussed it with me.

ARTHUR. We discussed it many times, dear.

CLARA. Well, I don't recall any such conversation.

ARTHUR. I know.

CLARA. What does Doctor Mader say about all this?

ARTHUR. Doctor Mader was our doctor when we lived in New York. We live in Florida now.

CLARA. I know that. Don't you think I know that?

ARTHUR. We haven't seen Doctor Mader for many years. I don't know how long, but many years now.

CLARA. Do you remember that sweater you had? The green one, with the collar sort of curled up, and the gold buttons down the front?

ARTHUR. I never had a sweater like that.

CLARA. Yes, and I asked you if the buttons were really gold, and you said yes, and you got them direct from the United States Mint.

ARTHUR. My God, Clara, you're talking about…we were children! How did you remember that sweater?

CLARA. And then, your father came and took us to the Circus at Madison Square Garden.

ARTHUR. The Garden was on Forty-Eighth Street then.

CLARA. Forty-ninth. And your father bought us ice cream and popcorn, and then he said, *(imitating)* "Now, you children should always tell the truth. But – you don't have to report everything that happens to 'The Mothers.' Popcorn and ice cream fall into that category."

ARTHUR. I must have been twelve, and you were ten. The girl next door.

CLARA. How is your father?

ARTHUR. *(rises)* Oh, my God! Do you hear yourself, Clara? My father's dead. He's been dead. He's dead.

CLARA. Well, you don't have to shout. He was a nice man and I should think you'd have a little more respect. Do you remember the time he took us to our first Broadway play? He just walked in and surprised us with the tickets.

ARTHUR. I remember.

CLARA. You said life was full of surprises. And that's the way you liked it. You said you didn't want to know what was coming next. I remember the day you surprised me with the engagement ring. And then later – out of the clear blue sky, we take off and spend a month in Europe.

ARTHUR. I'm afraid I've run out of surprises, Clara. I know what's coming now. And it just…keeps…coming…

CLARA. Oh, my goodness, why am I wearing this hat?

ARTHUR. I think you know why.

CLARA. If I knew why, why would I ask? Now, why am I wearing this hat?

ARTHUR. Because you are going to the Home today. And I'm going with you to see that you're settled. I won't let you go alone. I'll see that you're settled.

(**CLARA** *rises, crosses towards kitchen.*)

CLARA. Don't be silly. I'm not going to any Home. This is my home.

ARTHUR. They should have been here by now.

CLARA. Well, what do you want for supper?

ARTHUR. *(intercepting her)* You don't have to cook supper, Clara.

CLARA. Oh, I suppose it's going to cook itself.

ARTHUR. They're going to give you supper at the Home.

CLARA. I'm not going to the Home. This is my home. *(looking at her shoes)* My shoes are tight. They weren't tight before. Now they're tight.

ARTHUR. Maybe that's because –

CLARA. Maybe that's because what?

ARTHUR. Nothing.

CLARA. No...maybe that's because what?

ARTHUR. Because they were in the refrigerator overnight. Actually, in the freezer.

CLARA. Why did you put my shoes in the freezer, for heaven's sake?

ARTHUR. I didn't.

CLARA. Well then, who did?

ARTHUR. You did.

CLARA. Now you're just being ridiculous. I should know better than to listen to you. Silly. You're Mister Silly-Willy. I used to call you that when you did your George M. Cohan imitation.

ARTHUR. I never did a George M. Cohan imitation.

CLARA. All right, you did an imitation of James Cagney doing George M. Cohan. Don't try to trick me Mister Silly-Willy. Remember...

(sings)

GIVE MY REGARDS TO BROADWAY
La la la la la la la la
Come on…GIVE MY REGARDS…Come on, sing with
me.

(CLARA *crosses to* **ARTHUR**. *They both sing.)*

TOGETHER.
GIVE MY REGARDS TO BROADWAY

ARTHUR.
I NEVER COULD REMEMBER THIS LINE

TOGETHER.
TELL ALL THE GANG ON FORTY-SECOND STREET
THAT I WILL SOON BE THERE

(ARTHUR *looks at his watch.)*

CLARA. You needn't look at your watch. I'm not going to
the Home. I don't care if they come after me with a
straight jacket, I'm not going. *(sits)*

ARTHUR. Clara, my dear…no one is coming after you with a
straight jacket. No one is going to harm you…ever. *(He
takes her hand and sits next to her.)* But I can no longer
take care of you. Do you know that, my darling? I can
no longer take care of you. Try to understand that.

CLARA. So you're going to send me off to the Crazy House,
is that it?

ARTHUR. It's not a Crazy House. It's a Home, where they
can take care of you.

CLARA. And you decided this all by yourself?

ARTHUR. We discussed it many times. You just don't
remember.

CLARA. Why wasn't Neil brought in on this? As a matter of
fact, where is he now? You're about to put his mother
away, and you don't have the decency to consult with
our son?

ARTHUR. *(rises, crosses toward kitchen)* Clara…don't go on
like this.

CLARA. Because Neil is on my side, isn't he? And you can't
stand that. You're so anxious to send me to the Home;

you don't want Neil around to stop you. I know what's going on.

ARTHUR. Clara, please don't…

CLARA. I know what's going on. Call him. I want Neil here right now. *(beat)* Well, are you going to call him?

ARTHUR. Neil…Clara, Neil was killed in Vietnam…when he was just a boy. He came back in a coffin. We buried him, Clara. And they gave us a flag.

CLARA. *(crossing to him and striking him)* Liar! Liar! You are disgusting…to make up a story like that. Just so you can have your way. Liar! You Goddamn liar! I am not going to the Home – no matter what filthy lies you tell.

(**ARTHUR** *puts his arms around her, restraining her and taking her back to her chair. She's crying.*)

ARTHUR. It's all right. It's all right.

(Slowly, her tears subside and **ARTHUR** *offers her a handkerchief.)*

Here, take this.

CLARA. *(taking her own handkerchief)* Mine is cleaner.

(She dabs at her eyes and blows her nose. She smiles tentatively….)

You want to hear something silly?

ARTHUR. What?

CLARA. I don't know why I'm crying.

ARTHUR. It doesn't matter.

CLARA. But I'm not going to the Home. You promised.

ARTHUR. What did I promise? Do you remember?

CLARA. Yes, I do. I know I get confused sometimes, and I forget things…but the important things are inside me.

ARTHUR. What do you remember? I must know. Clara, you must tell me.

CLARA. Promises have been made here, and promises must be kept.

ARTHUR. Oh, my God – you do know.

(**CLARA** *goes to side table and takes a revolver out of the drawer. She crosses to* **ARTHUR** *and gives him the gun.)*

CLARA. Do it, Arthur.

(During below, **ARTHUR** *slowly crosses and stands behind* **CLARA**, *looking at the revolver.)*

CLARA. Do it. *(CLARA's tone changes to a frivolous babble as she sits on sofa.)* Promises are made to be kept. We certainly learned that my goodness when we were children. Remember the first New Year's Eve we spent together when we went to Times Square and it was so cold I promised then and there to knit you a pair of warm socks, and I certainly kept that promise even though one sock came up past your knee and the other one wouldn't even go over your ankle. And the time you came in from playing in the park with Neil and you were both so dirty DO IT, ARTHUR, DO IT!

*(***ARTHUR*** points the revolver at* **CLARA**'s *head.)*

ARTHUR. I can't! I can't! Forgive me, but I can't.

(He drops the gun on the sofa and turns away.)

I can't go through with it…and I can't keep you here. Don't you see that? You're going to the Home.

*(***CLARA*** rises, and she has the revolver in her hand. She points it at* **ARTHUR**.)*

CLARA. I am not going to the Home.

(She fires a SHOT! **ARTHUR** *falls.)*

I am not – going to the Home.

(She drops the revolver, looking vacantly out front. Then, slowly and haltingly, she sings…)

GIVE MY REGARDS TO BROADWAY
REMEMBER ME TO HERALD SQUARE
I got it! Arthur, you'll be proud of me. You couldn't remember it, but I did. Arthur…Arthur…Oh, where's he gone to now?

(She sits.)

REMEMBER ME TO HERALD SQUARE
TELL ALL THE GANG ON FORTY-SECOND STREET
THAT I WILL SOON BE THERE…

(LIGHTS fade.)

(BLACKOUT)

ACT III
"Harry"

Scene 1

(Apartment 304. Same apartment as the others, with change of furniture.)

*(**HARRY** is seated on a high stool, at the kitchen table. He is wearing a paper party hat and has a noisemaker in one hand. On the table is a cordless telephone and a birthday cake with one lit candle on it.)*

HARRY.

Happy birthday, Harry. Happy birthday to me.

*(**HARRY** uses the noisemaker.)*

Make a wish, Harry.

*(Blows out candle. Doorbell rings. **HARRY** picks up the phone.)*

Hello…Hell-ooo?

*(The doorbell rings again. **HARRY** speaks to the phone.)*

I knew it wasn't you.

(Puts phone down, crosses to front door and opens it.)

*(**MARK** enters carrying a case a little larger than a typewriter. He puts the case down, closing the door behind him, and hands **HARRY** his business card.)*

MARK. *(speaking slowly and loudly)* Mister Rossoff, my name is Mark Seagal. Here's my card. I am with the Florida Hearing Aid Center. You called us. You wanted a free test right in the comfort of your own home. Is that right?

HARRY. Why are you shouting? What kind of a test is it if you're going to stand there and shout? Christ, they could hear you back in New York.

MARK. Sorry, Mister Rossoff...but most of the people I meet need a little help, you know? You did want the test, didn't you?

HARRY. It is free isn't it? It says in the ad it's free.

MARK. Yes, sir, it's free. Now, sir, I'm going to set up here. Would you like to sit down and get comfortable?

(**HARRY** *sits on the high stool.*)

Wouldn't you be more comfortable in a chair?

HARRY. Nope. I always sit here.

MARK. Oh? Why is that?

HARRY. Habit.

MARK. Ah. *(He has picked up his machine and is looking about.)* May I put my equipment on the table?

HARRY. Sure, put the cake on the counter if there's not enough room.

MARK. *(as he moves the cake)* Somebody's birthday?

HARRY. Sure is. *(pointing to his paper hat)* Didn't you notice the hat when you came in?

MARK. As a matter of fact I did.

HARRY. You didn't say anything.

MARK. What you choose to wear in your own home, sir, is really none of my business. So I didn't say anything.

HARRY. That's a good answer. I like that. You managed to be polite, and still put this old codger in his place. And on my birthday, too.

MARK. Oh, I didn't know it was your birthday. There's only one candle on the cake.

HARRY. The last time I tried to put a candle on the cake for each year, the damn smoke alarm went off.

(**MARK** *puts a set of earphones from the machine over* **HARRY**'*s ears.*)

MARK. Is that comfortable? Now...you're going to hear a series of beeps. Sometimes in the right ear, and sometimes in the left. I want you to raise your right hand when you hear the beep in your right ear, and your left hand for the left ear. Do you understand that?

HARRY. I may be old, Sonny, but I'm not stupid.

MARK. *(He is pressing buttons on the machine.)* Did you hear that?

HARRY. Yeah. What was that?

MARK. That was the beep. It can be a little confusing at first. How's that?

> *(**HARRY**'s left hand goes up.)*

Good. And now?

> *(**HARRY**'s left hand goes up again.)*

Good. And now?

> *(**HARRY**'s right hand goes up.)*

Good. Now you're going to hear the signal in your right ear. It will be getting weaker and weaker. I want you to keep your right hand up, and put it down when you can no longer hear the signal.

> *(**HARRY**'s right hand goes up, stays as **MARK** pushes buttons, then comes down. **MARK** makes notes on a sheet of paper.)*

That's fine. Now the left hand.

HARRY. *(pointing to his earphones)* Can you get me out of this for a minute? I have to leave the room.

> *(**MARK** removes earphones from **HARRY**. **HARRY** crosses to Downstage left door.)*

MARK. No problem. Take your time.

HARRY. I'll only be a second.

> *(**HARRY** exits. **MARK** looks around the apartment. **HARRY** enters from same door in a surprisingly short time.)*

MARK. That was fast.

HARRY. Gas. *(crosses to his stool)* I hate to fart in front of company.

> *(**HARRY** resumes his seat on the stool. **MARK** replaces the earphones on **HARRY**.)*

MARK. Nice place you have here. You live alone?

HARRY. Yep.

MARK. Must be great to have two bedrooms. All the space you need. Now where I live…

HARRY. One bedroom. I only have one bedroom

MARK. But there are two doors – sure looks like two bed-rooms.

HARRY. Smart architect. He put in two nice looking doors to make the place look bigger. *(points to the door he used)* That one's a closet.

MARK. Oh. A closet. Now you're going to hear the signal in your left ear. Please keep your left hand up until you can no longer hear the beeps.

*(**HARRY** raises his left hand, and lowers it after a few seconds.)*

Good…good. We'll send you a copy of your report next week.

*(**MARK** takes the earphones off **HARRY** and starts to pack up his machine.)*

HARRY. Is that it?

MARK. There is another part, but – well, I have several appointments today and, from what I can tell, you're in good shape.

HARRY. I'm entitled to the full test.

MARK. You're right sir. For the second part, I'm going to stand behind you…no, don't look at me – look straight ahead…we don't want any lip reading. I want you to repeat the words or sentences that I say. But first, I'd like to ask you a question…

HARRY. Fire away.

MARK. Why did you fart in the closet? Another habit?

HARRY. Now it's a habit. But there's a reason why it started.

MARK. Would you care to explain?

HARRY. Might take a little time. I thought you were in a hurry to get out of here.

MARK. For this, I'll stay.

HARRY. It started with Charity. That's my daughter, Charity... ha!

MARK. I take it you don't like Charity?

HARRY. She's a witch! See, when I retired – that was twenty-seven years ago, on my birthday – and I'm eighty-nine today...

MARK. My God. Happy Birthday! And many happy returns.

HARRY. Thank you, but there aren't going to be many returns – happy or otherwise. I'm only living to spite my daughter. But this past year I had two heart attacks, so I don't see that I can outlive her.

MARK. Today people live many years with a heart condition.

HARRY. Oh, don't I wish. Anyway, shortly after I retired, my wife died. But before she died she made me promise to take care of Charity. "She's our flesh and blood, and blood is thicker than water," she said. Then Charity came sniffin' around. Not because her mother died, but because she expected me to follow. You know what they say...when one partner goes, the other one follows. And that's all she wanted. She figured I took early retirement – she should have early inheritance.

MARK. You can't be sure of that.

HARRY. I'm sure! I'm sure! You know what she did last year? She took me to court. Tried to prove me incompetent. Incompetent to handle my own affairs. She wanted to put her hands on the money, don't you see?

MARK. Mister Rossoff, you're getting too excited. Keep this up and you'll play right into her hands...know what I mean? You could drop dead right now.

HARRY. Say, you're all right. And call me Harry.

MARK. Okay, Harry.

HARRY. Okay, Mark.

MARK. So Harry...Why did you fart in the closet?

HARRY. It started years ago – about the time she was hinting I should turn over my money to her – she started coming to visit and poking her nose all over the apartment. I'd find out later she went though every drawer in the house, even the kitchen. But the closet!...she seemed to have a special thing for the closet.

MARK. What did she expect to find?

HARRY. I don't know. All I keep in that closet is sweaters. Christ, I wear a sweater maybe three or four times a year, and I have thirty-nine sweaters in that closet. Anyway, when I knew she was coming, I started farting in the closet. Then, after a while I started laying a few in there in case she'd show up unexpected. And then...well...

MARK. You were hooked. Okay. Let's get back to the test. (*He resumes his position behind* **HARRY**.) Repeat the words or sentences you hear.

HARRY. That husband of hers, Walter Pipick, is a lawyer, you know. They don't even have to pay court costs...

MARK. Hothouse.

HARRY. What?

MARK. You didn't hear me?

HARRY. I heard you. You said hothouse.

MARK. Right. Now, can we go ahead? Drawbridge.

HARRY. Drawbridge.

MARK. Fishing is a very popular sport.

HARRY. Fishing is a very popular sport.

MARK. Please throw out that pile of trash.

HARRY. I'd throw them both out – but they're just waiting for me to make a false move, and then back to court we go.

MARK. Harry. Do you want me to finish the test?

HARRY. Sorry.

MARK. To live well is the best revenge.

HARRY. To live well is the best revenge.

MARK. The wind is fine for flying a kite.

HARRY. To live well is the best revenge! I love it!

MARK. Okay that's it. We really don't have to go any further.

HARRY. Mark, I'll take one of your hearing aid gadgets. Don't you see? That's what I've been missing.

MARK. A hearing aid?

HARRY. To live well is the best revenge! I was concentrating on getting at her. All I have to do is live It up, and she goes down the drain.

MARK. Why don't you just cut her out of your will?

HARRY. I told you. I promised my wife. Now, how much are one of your gadgets?

MARK. A hearing aid? Well, depends…about two thousand dollars.

HARRY. Put me down for two.

MARK. I can't do that, Harry.

HARRY. Why not?

MARK. You don't have a hearing problem.

HARRY. But I have other problems. And I think you gave me the answer to my biggest problem. To live well is the best revenge! The least I can do is buy a couple of your hearing gadgets.

MARK. No way, Harry.

HARRY. You really mean that, don't you?

MARK. Yes sir, I do.

HARRY. Well, I'll be damned. I'll be double damned. Mark, have a birthday drink with me. You can't refuse me that.

*(**HARRY** crosses to behind kitchen counter and produces a bottle of Brandy.)*

MARK. Of course not, Harry.

*(**HARRY** fills two shot glasses with Brandy, hands one to **MARK**.)*

HARRY. We're going to make a special toast.

MARK. Well, happy birthday.

HARRY. No wait. We're drinking to something else. In this world of greed and larceny…I'll drink to a rare find – Mark Seagal. *(He sips at his glass.)* And I owe you an apology.

MARK. What for?

HARRY. I called in on the ad for the hearing test…well, just to pass the time. I have to think of different things to pass the time. There's nothing wrong with my hearing.

MARK. I knew that two minutes after I was in the door.

HARRY. Then why…?

MARK. This is not the first time this has happened. And whenever I'm in this situation…what the hell, I give a little time to a person who's all alone. What are you looking at me like that for? It's the only thing I have to give.

HARRY. *(holding up his glass)* To a rare find, indeed…

MARK. Happy Birthday, Harry.

(They drink.)

HARRY. I can see me on one of them cruises. Best cabin on the ship…invited to the Captain's table…white dinner jacket. Whoops, I'll need a new wardrobe. This is exciting, Mark. This is the first time I've been excited about anything in years.

MARK. That's great. I think life is something to be excited about. Something to enjoy.

HARRY. Right. And there's another thing I would enjoy. Maybe you can help me with this…

MARK. I will if I can, Harry.

HARRY. Good. You can help me get a hooker.

MARK. A what?

HARRY. They got a new word for it? They used to call 'em hookers.

MARK. They still do.

HARRY. See? I got it right.

MARK. Come on, Harry – act your age.

HARRY. Damnit, I am acting my age. I've got no time for a romance. I need a hooker.

MARK. Well I don't know any hookers.

HARRY. Well ain't we the friggin' goody-two-shoes. You must know somebody who knows somebody who knows a hooker.

MARK. Happy Birthday, Harry. I've got to go now.

*(**MARK** picks up his case, and crosses to front door with **HARRY** behind him. He opens the front door and turns into the room.)*

MARK. Hey, Harry, it's been nice meeting you. You've got my number. If there's anything I can do for you – anything legitimate – call me.

HARRY. Okay, okay.

(They shake hands.)

HARRY. Mark, you made it a nice birthday for me. Now, I'm going to shut the door, turn off the phone…and to hell with the whole world.

*(**MARK** exits, and **HARRY** lingers in the doorway. He waves once, then turns slowly into the room, pulling the door behind him. Just before the door is closed, it is pulled open from the outside and **CHARITY** and **WALTER PIPICK** come bursting in. **CHARITY** has a gift-wrapped box, which she thrusts towards **HARRY**, who ignores it.)*

CHARITY. Happy Birthday Daddy dear.

WALTER. Happy Birthday Daddy dear.

HARRY. *(looking out front)* Oh shit!

*(**CHARITY** now forcing the gift box on **HARRY**.)*

CHARITY. Hold this, Daddy dear. I have to go to the bathroom something awful.

(She exits through the bedroom door.)

WALTER. Well, Daddy dear, how's it feel to be eighty-nine?

HARRY. Why don't you cut that out?

*(**HARRY** crosses and sits on his stool.)*

WALTER. Just trying to make a civil conversation.

HARRY. As in Civil Court?

WALTER. Oh come on, Daddy – that was last year. Nothing came of it anyway.

HARRY. That wasn't your fault.

WALTER. That's not the way Charity puts it.

(**CHARITY** *enters from bedroom door and exits into closet door.*)

HARRY. You know, I used to think of you as a credit to your profession. A man with some judgment…

WALTER. Yes?

HARRY. So how could you live with my daughter all these years?

(**CHARITY** *comes out of the closet holding a handkerchief over her nose and coughing.*)

CHARITY. My God, my God…something's got to be done. Aren't you going to open your present Daddy dear? *(to* **WALTER***)* I tell you it's getting worse.

WALTER. Why do you go in there, then?

CHARITY. He's hiding something in there. He wouldn't do that unless he was hiding something in there. What are you hiding in there, Daddy dear?

(**HARRY** *opens his present.*)

HARRY. None of your business!

WALTER. Why don't you two cut it out?

HARRY. Just what I needed. A sweater.

(**HARRY** *holds up a sweater he has taken from the box.*)

CHARITY. You're welcome, Daddy dear.

WALTER. Slip it on, if you want to…we're taking you to dinner.

HARRY. Oh no you're not.

CHARITY. Yes we are.

HARRY. No you're not.

CHARITY. Well, for heaven's sake why not.

HARRY. Because, every time you take me out to dinner, I have to pick up the check. That cheap bastard husband of yours has his pockets glued together…

CHARITY. He is not cheap, Daddy dear. It's just that things have been difficult in the financial department lately…

WALTER. I'm picking up the check tonight. You can count on that.

HARRY. *(glances at his watch)* Well, you'd better hurry up, Sonny – you can still catch the early bird. But without me.

WALTER. Actually, there are a few things we'd like to discuss at dinner...

HARRY. Such as?

CHARITY. Such as why don't you let Walter handle your finances? He's doing it for other clients...and very successfully too.

HARRY. That's why he hasn't picked up one lousy dinner tab in ten years.

CHARITY. And then, he's got this marvelous real estate investment...If you put one or two hundred thousand up now, in a few years there'll be just oodles of money for you.

HARRY. Oodles of money for who?

CHARITY. For you, Daddy dear.

HARRY. I don't have to come to dinner – I think I'm going to throw up right now.

WALTER. I told you he was impossible. He won't even listen.

CHARITY. You're getting me angry, Daddy dear. Very angry indeed! I'm going to have to leave you alone, that's all. All alone on your birthday! Come, Walter.

(**CHARITY** *and* **WALTER** *exit.*)

HARRY. Happy Birthday to me! *(blows noisemaker)*

(BLACKOUT)

Scene 2

(It is three days later. **HARRY** *is seated on his stool watching* **MARK** *pace the floor.)*

MARK. I don't know how I let you talk me into this. It's stupid…just stupid!

HARRY. Why, for God's sake? I didn't have a contact – you made a contact for me.

MARK. But for Christ's sake you're eighty-nine years old. You shouldn't be running around with a hooker.

HARRY. I'm not going to run around with her. I can't even walk fast.

MARK. Then what are you going to do with her, Harry?

HARRY. Same thing everybody else does.

MARK. You sure about that?

HARRY. No…but I'm going to find out. I hope she's a nice person. Did Charlie say if she was a nice person?

MARK. Charlie said she is class. He didn't comment on whether or not she was a nice person.

HARRY. And you didn't ask?

MARK. I don't want to be responsible for this, Harry. You asked me to make a contact…I found this guy Charlie – knows a million girls, he says. So I explained the situation to him, and he's sending someone over at…*(He looks at his watch.)*…oh my gosh, it's after three. She should have been here by now. I have to go.

HARRY. No you don't. You promised!

MARK. Alright. I won't leave you now. But I'm not responsible if she's not a nice person.

HARRY. Okay.

MARK. And I'm not responsible if you don't like her.

HARRY. Okay.

MARK. And I'm certainly not responsible if you end up with a venereal disease.

HARRY. Hold it – hold it right there. Is there something you're not telling me?

MARK. Harry, there's nothing I'm not telling you. Are you sure you're ready for this?

HARRY. What do I have to get ready?

MARK. I mean, do you have a prophylactic?

HARRY. I don't think so.

MARK. I'm talking about a condom.

HARRY. A bag?

MARK. A rubber.

HARRY. That's a bag. Why don't you say what you mean, for Christ sake!

MARK. Well, do you have one?

HARRY. No.

MARK. I thought you might not.

(**MARK** *hands* **HARRY** *a small envelope with a "Trojan" prophylactic in it.*)

MARK. Here, take this.

HARRY. Look at that – same people still in business after all these years. That's the kind of thing you should get into.

MARK. No thanks. I'm into my own thing – I sell hearing aids, remember?

HARRY. Of course I remember. How many did you sell this week?

MARK. None.

HARRY. *(indicating the packet)* I bet these babies sell like hotcakes.

MARK. I'm doing all right. I've been seeing new prospects the last few days. What have you been up to?

HARRY. I'm buying. Buying, buying. I bought a brand new wardrobe. It's being tailored for Harry the sheik even as we speak. I'm looking into cruises. And I bought a globe. It's made out of gold and silver.

MARK. You don't need a globe.

HARRY. That's the idea. I get a bang out of it when I really don't need what I'm buying.

(The doorbell rings.)

HARRY. It's her…it's her.

MARK. Well, aren't you going to answer the door?

HARRY. I…I can't. It'll take too long. You answer it.

> (**MARK** *crosses and opens the door.* **CHI CHI** *steps into the room.)*

CHI CHI. Hello, darling, you are lookin' at Chi Chi La Boo Boo!

> *(There is silence as she stands posing.)*

HARRY. She's perfect.

MARK. I'm Mark – Mark Seagal. I sell hearing aids.

CHI CHI. Well ain't that sweet. Guess what I sell?

HARRY. Oh boy! Oh boy-o-boy-o-boy!

MARK. But…but…but…but…

CHI CHI. Hey, as soon as you can stop percolatin, we're gonna make pretty music together. You're kind of cute. *(She takes in* **HARRY** *with her eyes.)* What's he gonna do – watch?

HARRY. I'm the John.

MARK. What?

HARRY. I'm the John. That's what they call 'em, right Chi Chi?

CHI CHI. That's what they call 'em, Grandpa.

HARRY. The name's Harry.

CHI CHI. You payin' for this here party?

HARRY. Yep.

CHI CHI. You just got cuter than him, Harry.

HARRY. Excuse me.

> (**HARRY** *hurries to closet door and exits.)*

CHI CHI. Does he want me to follow him into the bedroom?

> *(She starts to follow.)*

MARK. I wouldn't go in there if I were you.

CHI CHI. Why not.

MARK. It's too long a story. He'll be out in a sec-

(HARRY enters.)

MARK. There he is.

HARRY. Where were we?

CHI CHI. You were sayin' that you're payin' for this party.

HARRY. Oh...right. I'll take care of the finances.

CHI CHI. You know what they say, Harry...business before pleasure. Why don't we settle the finances right now. That'll be a hundred dollars. Cash.

HARRY. No problem.

(HARRY crosses behind kitchen counter and gets money jar.)

CHI CHI. Or I accept all major credit cards.

MARK. A hundred dollars! That's highway robbery!

CHI CHI. How much did you think it was, sport?

MARK. Oh...I don't know...I thought maybe twenty dollars.

CHI CHI. Twenty dollars! I leave that much in the poor box at church.

HARRY. I knew she was a nice person.

(He counts as he hands money to CHI CHI.)

Forty, sixty, eighty...ninety...ninety-five...ninety-six... ninety-seven...eight...nine...

(doling out change) and a hundred...right?

CHI CHI. I've never seen anybody do that. But okay...you took care of business, now I do my thing. Let's go Grandpa.

HARRY. I wish you wouldn't call me that.

CHI CHI. You're a paid up member, sweetie. I'll call you anything you want – Harry. Can we go now...Harry?

MARK. I still say that's a lot of money...

CHI CHI. Hey...hey...Chi Chi comes with a guarantee. Full satisfaction or your money back. Now, butt out, Buster!

(CHI CHI takes HARRY's hand, starts for closet door.)

HARRY. Yeah, butt out, Buster! *(to CHI CHI)* Wrong door, Chi Chi. It's this one.

MARK. Okay, I'll butt out. As a matter of fact, I'm leaving.

(HARRY leads CHI CHI to the bedroom door, and turns to MARK.)

HARRY. No, no. You promised to stay.

CHI CHI. Hang out, big guy, there's enough to go around for everyone.

MARK. Okay…I'll hang out a couple of minutes.

HARRY. It's going to take a lot more than that. A lot more.

(HARRY takes CHI CHI by the hand, and they exit. CHI CHI leans her head back into the room.)

CHI CHI. A couple of minutes.

(She exits. MARK starts pacing the floor. MARK crosses to table, picks up condom HARRY has left on the table, crosses to the bedroom door, gets ready to knock, but hesitates. Just as he decides to knock, the front door opens. MARK puts condom in his shirt pocket and crosses towards front door. CHARITY and WALTER come busting in.)

CHARITY. Yoo-hoo, Daddy Dear. Who are you? Where's my father? What have you done with him?

MARK. I haven't done anything with him.

CHARITY. Never mind that – just answer the question.

MARK. What question?

CHARITY. Who are you? Walter, call the police.

WALTER. I'm sure the gentleman can tell us who he is.

MARK. I'm Mark Seagal. Who are you?

WALTER. We're Mister and Missus Pipick.

MARK. Walter Pipick? Oh, then you're Charity?

WALTER. *(to CHARITY)* See? He knows us.

CHARITY. This doesn't explain what you're doing here, Mister Whatever-your-name-is.

MARK. What am I doing here…I'm with Florida Hearing Aid Center…here's my card…

(MARK reaches in his pocket and hands CHARITY the condom. As CHARITY. stares in puzzlement, he plucks it out of her hand.)

MARK. Oops!

(MARK searches pockets for his card and hands it to CHARITY.)

CHARITY. My father doesn't have a hearing problem.

MARK. We'll determine that soon enough. I'm here to give him a test.

CHARITY. So, where is he?

MARK. He's in the bedroom…resting.

CHARITY. For a hearing test? That's nonsense. I'll go get him.

(CHARITY starts for bedroom door.)

MARK. I wouldn't do that… *(He shouts toward the bedroom door.)* MRS. PIPICK…MRS. CHARITY PIPICK.

CHARITY. I'm not deaf. Why shouldn't I get my father.

MARK. He's put drops in his ears…acetylsalicylic acid. Now if you cause an imbalance…if he gets up suddenly… well…I won't be responsible for what may happen. He shouldn't even stand up for the next…oh…half an hour – at least.

WALTER. Certainly sounds like a complicated test.

MARK. Thorough, Mr. Pipick. We think of it as thorough.

(HARRY enters from bedroom smiling.)

HARRY. Well…well, isn't this nice. I see I have visitors.

MARK. I would say you have a houseful.

CHARITY. Daddy dear, what are you doing on your feet?

HARRY. I walk this way. See?

(HARRY crosses to the counter.)

CHARITY. But what about the drops in your ears?

HARRY. What the hell are you talking about? I didn't get one drop in my ear.

MARK. Oh, you didn't put the drops in your ears – the drops I gave you – you didn't put them in your ears?

HARRY. Has everybody gone crazy? Just because I –

(**HARRY** *points toward the bedroom.*)

CHARITY. Just because you what?

HARRY. It's not important.

CHARITY. Something is going on in that bedroom…

HARRY. Yes. Charity, the time has come for me to have a frank talk with you…

CHARITY. I don't like this.

HARRY. In that bedroom…in that bedroom is a woman –

CHARITY. A woman?

HARRY. …and I've been consorting with that woman.

CHARITY. *(to **WALTER**)* Do you know what he's saying?

WALTER. If he's saying what I think he's saying, then I know what he's saying.

CHARITY. What are we going to do about this?

WALTER. There's nothing *to* do. And anyway, what's the harm?

HARRY. I'm going to get married.

CHARITY. That's the harm! That's the harm! Daddy dear, we have to talk. We have to consider this very carefully…*don't* we Walter?

WALTER. Oh yes. A thing like this could be hazardous to your health.

HARRY. Don't you wish…and hopefully before the ceremony.

WALTER. You've got us all wrong, Daddy.

CHARITY. And when are we going to meet this fine lady who sneaks into your bedroom and is only after your money anyway?

HARRY. You shouldn't make up your mind about people you haven't even met, Charity. That's not the way I brought you up. Now if you want to meet the lady on a fair and open-minded basis…fine, I'll arrange that.

CHARITY. When?

HARRY. Right now.

CHARITY. Agreed, Daddy dear…let's meet her.

(**HARRY** *crosses towards bedroom door.*)

MARK. You sure you want to do this, Harry?

CHARITY. *(to* **MARK***)* You stay out of this.

MARK. Right.

(**MARK** *sits by counter and pours himself a drink.* **HARRY** *knocks on bedroom door.*)

HARRY. My dear, would you like to come out now? *(No answer. He knocks again.)* Please…my daughter would like to meet you.

(**CHI CHI** *enters and poses.*)

CHI CHI. Hello, darling, you are lookin' at Chi Chi La Boo Boo!

CHARITY. Oh my God!

HARRY. Chi Chi, this is my daughter, Charity. Charity, say hello to my fiancée…

CHI CHI. His fiancée…

CHARITY. This is not happening. *(looks up)* Tell me this is not happening.

HARRY. And this is my son-in-law, Walter.

CHARITY. *(to* **WALTER***)* You can wake me up now, Walter… Walter!

WALTER. We're both wide awake I'm afraid.

CHARITY. Then go over to that…that thing and tell her to get out of here and never come back again.

WALTER. I can't do that. There's no legal ground.

CHARITY. You pick *now* to be a lawyer? All right, all right. Make a bargain…a compromise. Offer her money. Do something.

(**HARRY** *crosses to* **CHARITY** *as* **WALTER** *crosses to* **CHI CHI***.*)

HARRY. Well, now that you've met her, what do you think?

CHARITY. I need a drink.

HARRY. Oh, sure. Good idea. Sort of a celebration.

(MARK *pours* CHARITY *a drink as they gather by the counter.* WALTER *approaches* CHI CHI.)

CHI CHI. Well, well, I thought you'd never recognize your old friend Chi Chi.

WALTER. *(signals for* CHI CHI *to be quiet)* Shhh! That's my wife over there.

CHI CHI. Well how lucky can you get!

WALTER. Look, Chi Chi...it would be best for everyone concerned if you just left quietly – right now.

CHI CHI. Listen, Buster, Harry hired me, and Harry is the only one who can tell me to leave. It's a matter of ethics.

WALTER. It's a matter of money, and we can talk about that. But not right now. I'll call you. Give me your number.

(WALTER *takes out a pad and pencil, prepares to take down number.*)

CHI CHI. 1-800...

(Pause as WALTER *looks at her, then back to his pad.)*

555-SCREW.

(WALTER *crosses to* CHARITY.)

CHARITY. Well, what does she want?

WALTER. She wouldn't tell me.

CHARITY. Get me out of here. I can't take any more.

(CHARITY *and* WALTER *cross to front door.*)

CHARITY. I don't know what you're up to Daddy dear, Daddy dear, but you're not going to get away with it! I'll be back when you get rid of that...that thing...that creature – I don't even know what to call her!

CHI CHI. You can call me Mother.

CHARITY. That's it, Walter. Out – get me out!

(CHARITY *and* WALTER *exit.*)

HARRY. I never had such a good time in my life. *(to* CHI CHI, *imitating her)* You can call me Mother...

(They all laugh.)

CHI CHI. Okay...we had our laugh. Now, I gotta go out and find some work.

MARK. Are you busy these days?

CHI CHI. I do all right with the cholesterol crowd. Here Harry...

(She has taken money out of her purse and is counting it out to HARRY.*)*

...ninety-nine...

(She counts out change.)...twenty-five...fifty...seventy-five...one hundred.

HARRY. Keep it, Chi Chi. You're more than worth it.

CHI CHI. No good, Harry. I told you Chi Chi comes with a guarantee...in case of a strike-out, your money is cheerfully refunded.

(She crosses to front door.)

MARK. *(to* HARRY*)* After all that – you struck out?

HARRY. I decided to let sleeping dogs lie.

CHI CHI. *(as she exits)* Sleeping dogs I can wake up...But Grandpa...that little puppy is dead.

(HARRY *starts laughing, a giggle at first, then louder and louder into uncontrollable laughter.)*

(MARK *pauses as he observes* HARRY.*)*

MARK. Harry, you're turning blue. Stop it.

(HARRY *suddenly stiffens and falls face down on the couch.)*

Oh my God!

(He crosses to HARRY, *feels for a pulse in* HARRY*'s neck, finds none.)*

(BLACKOUT)

Scene 3

(It is two days later. The apartment is dark. We hear the lock turn on the door, and **CHARITY** *and* **WALTER** *enter. They are dressed more formally than usual.)*

CHARITY. Now where is that light switch…

WALTER. No, a little higher. There it is.

(LIGHTS on. Sitting on his customary stool is **HARRY**.*)*

CHARITY. Well, it's over. Finally, finally over! I thought it would take forever.

WALTER. Actually, I thought the funeral went quite smoothly. I didn't know the old boy had so many friends.

HARRY. How many were there?

CHARITY. A bunch of old foggies and misfits, if you ask me.

HARRY. How many?

WALTER. There must have been two hundred people there – maybe more. They couldn't all have been misfits.

CHARITY. That's right, take his side. Just like you did in the lawyer's office.

WALTER. Well, the reading of the Will is no time to call your father a shit.

CHARITY. Well, he is. Did he have to keep saying blood is thicker than water?

WALTER. What's the difference? We got the money, didn't we?

CHARITY. I got the money, don't forget that. I got the money. It's mine. I've been waiting all my life for this.

HARRY. I always said that.

WALTER. Your father always said that. He always said you were after the money.

CHARITY. Well, for once he was right. *(looking up)* Did you hear that Daddy dear? You were right. Bingo!

WALTER. *(approaching the couch)* Here's where it happened. He just keeled over and he was gone. But they said he died laughing.

CHARITY. Must have been some joke. *(looking around)* I don't suppose we can get much for the furniture, but I'll auction it off or give it away, and then put the apartment up for sale.

WALTER. You can't sell the apartment.

HARRY. He's right.

CHARITY. Why can't I?

WALTER. You heard the stipulation in the Will. You have to live in the apartment for three years before you get the money. If you don't, the estate goes to "Meals on Wheels."

CHARITY. I wouldn't live in this dump for three minutes. You have to get me out of this.

WALTER. And how am I supposed to do that?

CHARITY. You're the lawyer. Think of something.

WALTER. I may be a lawyer, but I'm not a...a...

HARRY. Magician.

WALTER. ...magician. You have to live up to all the stipulations in the Will, or you don't get the money.

CHARITY. Alright, what if we stay where we are. Who would know I'm not living here?

HARRY. Tell her, Walter.

WALTER. Your father was not a stupid man. Jason Lesko is a good lawyer, and he's also the Executor of the estate.

CHARITY. So?

WALTER. Jason told me they've set aside a sum of money for surveillance.

CHARITY. What does that mean? They're going to treat me like some common criminal? Oh how I hate that man. I hate him. I'm almost tempted to walk away from this whole thing.

HARRY. But you won't.

CHARITY. But I won't.

WALTER. Jason told me they're going to be checking up on you from time to time. We'll never know when. If they determine that this is not your main domicile, well... that's it.

CHARITY. *(pacing)* I'll figure a way to beat him. Is it cold in here?

HARRY. Why don't you get a sweater?

(CHARITY stops pacing as she comes to a decision.)

CHARITY. Wait a minute. I've got it. Here's what I'll do. I'll get rid of everything that's in here. The furniture, the rugs, the pictures...everything that would remind me of that man. Can I do that?

WALTER. I don't see why not.

CHARITY. Legally?

WALTER. Yes, legally.

CHARITY. Then that's it. I'll redecorate this place from top to bottom. There won't be a trace of that man in this apartment. Then, I'll sit and wait for the money to roll in.

WALTER. Now that's a sensible decision. I knew I could count on you.

CHARITY. Not a trace. *(beat)* It is getting cold in here.

HARRY. Why don't you get a sweater?

WALTER. Tell you what. I'll make us a drink. That'll warm you up. Then, I'm taking you out to dinner.

CHARITY. Good.

(WALTER crosses behind counter.)

WALTER. There was a bottle of Scotch back here, if I'm not mistaken.

CHARITY. I think I will get a sweater.

(CHARITY crosses to closet with HARRY close behind her. They both enter closet. WALTER has found Scotch and is pouring drinks. CHARITY comes out of the closet gagging and holding a handkerchief to her nose. HARRY is close behind amd crosses to stool.)

CHARITY. Oh my God! Oh my God! Wal-ter...WAL-TER.. Get me out of here. Now! I can't spend another minute in this place – let alone three years. Oh, I would never make THREE YEARS!

WALTER. I don't understand. What happened?

CHARITY. He's here. The son-of-a-bitch is here!

WALTER. Wait, Charity, the money will go to "Meals on Wheels."

*(***CHARITY*** *and* ***WALTER*** *exit.)*

HARRY. My favorite Charity!

*(***HARRY*** *grins in triumph at the audience.)*

(CURTAIN)

Curtain Call Music – "OLD IS IN"

OLD IS IN
GOLLY GEE
OLD IS THE LATEST THING TO BE
SO WRINKLE YOUR SKIN
OLD IS IN

OLD IS US
ROLL THE DRUM
WE'RE AN IDEA WHOSE TIME HAS COME
HALF FARE ON THE BUS
OLD IS US

SO WHAT IF THE COPS KEEP GETTING YOUNGER
EVERY DAY
SO WHAT IF THE BATHROOM DOOR GETS
FARTHER AND FARTHER AWAY
WHO CARES IF YOUR FAVORITE DISHES GIVE YOU
INDIGESTION
AND IF LONG TERM BONDS ARE OUT OF THE
QUESTION

OLD IS IN
IT'S THE RAGE
NOW IS THE TIME TO FLAUNT YOUR AGE
LIKE WHISKEY AND SIN
OLD IS IN

SO PUT IN YOUR UPPERS AND GRIN
TUNE IN TO IRVING BERLIN
LIFE IS ABOUT TO BEGIN
OLD IS IN

OLD IS IN

WORDS + MUSIC BY
HUGO PERETTI
LUIGI CREATORE
GEORGE DAVID WEISS

1. OLD IS IN, GOL-LY GEE! OLD IS THE LA-TEST
2. OLD IS IN, ROLL THE DRUM. WE'RE AN I-DEA WHOSE

1. THING TO BE SO WRIN-KLE YOUR SKIN OLD IS IN—
2. TIME HAS COME HALF-FARE ON THE BUS

OLD IS US!

SO WHAT IF THE COPS KEEP GET-TING YOUNG-ER EV'RY DAY—

—? SO WHAT IF THE BATHROOM DOOR GETS FAR-THER AND FAR-THER A-

From the Reviews of
FLAMINGO COURT...

"'The Golden Girls' meets Neil Simon's *Plaza Suite*."
- AM New York

"A NEW HIT!" -
"Eyewitness News," WABC

"HILARIOUS COMEDY! THE PLAY IS HYSTERICAL. Jamie Farr &
Anita Gillette are sensational! I'm coming back again!"
- Joe Franklin, Bloomberg Radio

"A WALL-TO-WALL HOOT FOR OLD AND YOUNG ALIKE. THE
AUDIENCE LAUGHED UP A FLORIDA-WORTHY HURRICANE!
There are wonderful performances by the spirited Jamie Farr and the
adorable Anita Gillette and from Lucy Martin, Herbert Rubens and
Joe Vincent. *Flamingo Court*, funny enough even for young audiences,
is highly recommended to those between 60 and 80. Those above 80,
however, should be careful lest they laugh themselves to death. But, as
they themselves would surely agree, what a way to go!"
- John Simon, Bloomberg

"LICENSE TO KILL...WITH LAUGHTER. YOU'LL BE IN
HEAVEN with this trio of vignettes written by Luigi Creatore. The
cast has as much fun as the audience!"
- Associated Press

"FUNNY AND TOUCHING. With more than a few elements of
"The Golden Girls" and "The Sopranos," the play looks at the
choices, responsibilities and lasting legacies that come with age."
– *The Epoch Times*

"*Flamingo Court* knows its prime audience and plays to it skillfully.
Luigi Creatore springs his surprises expertly."
- *The New York Times*

"HILARIOUS COMEDY! I LAUGHED, I CRIED. Jamie Farr
certainly hasn't lost his comic touch."
- Jane Waldman, AP Radio

"NEIL SIMON-ESQUE!"
- *Associated Press*

"Hilarious! Jamie farr is lighting up the stage."
- CBS 2 News, WCBS TV

"A funny three-part comedy about the older generation"
- WOR Radio

OTHER TITLES AVAILABLE FROM SAMUEL FRENCH

EURYDICE
Sarah Ruhl

Dramatic Comedy / 5m, 2f / Unit Set

In *Eurydice*, Sarah Ruhl reimagines the classic myth of Orpheus through the eyes of its heroine. Dying too young on her wedding day, Eurydice must journey to the underworld, where she reunites with her father and struggles to remember her lost love. With contemporary characters, ingenious plot twists, and breathtaking visual effects, the play is a fresh look at a timeless love story.

"RHAPSODICALLY BEAUTIFUL. A weird and wonderful new play - an inexpressibly moving theatrical fable about love, loss and the pleasures and pains of memory."
- The New York Times

"EXHILARATING!! A luminous retelling of the Orpheus myth, lush and limpid as a dream where both author and audience swim in the magical, sometimes menacing, and always thrilling flow of the unconscious."
- *The New Yorker*

"Exquisitely staged by Les Waters and an inventive design team… Ruhl's wild flights of imagination, some deeply affecting passages and beautiful imagery provide transporting pleasures. They conspire to create original, at times breathtaking, stage pictures."
- *Variety*

"Touching, inventive, invigoratingly compact and luminously liquid in its rhythms and design, *Eurydice* reframes the ancient myth of ill-fated love to focus not on the bereaved musician but on his dead bride – and on her struggle with love beyond the grave as both wife and daughter."
- *The San Francisco Chronicle*

SAMUELFRENCH.COM